HINNOM MAGAZINE

JUNE 2017
ISSUE 001

Edited by C.P. Dunphey

Gehenna & Hinnom Books

Table of Contents:

Introduction

by C.P. Dunphey

Welcome to Gehenna & Hinnom.

In this manuscript, you will find some of the most interesting and promising voices in the genres of science fiction, horror, and fantasy. We hope to provide you, the readers, with quality fiction bi-monthly for as long as we can muster. Hopefully, this entails many years—and if we are being optimistic, decades—worth of short stories.

Science fiction is the only genre that begs the question, "*What if?*"

Horror is the only genre that is defined and titled after a human emotion.

Fantasy is the only genre that solely relies on world-building and imaginative creativity to captivate audiences.

Many see these genres as "genre-fiction," often reluctant to include them within the realms of "literature." It is our hope that we can prove the naysayers wrong. For what would "literature" be without such works as *Frankenstein*, *Dune*, or *The Lord of the Rings*?

What started out as a passion project has evolved into something magnificent and wondrous. Never in all my years of writing and editing, have I ever had such an amazing experience, as I have with building the foundations of Gehenna & Hinnom. We have encountered some of the most talented authors in the world since we opened our doors a few months ago, and the great adventure has only just begun.

However, all my useless editing and brain-turning-to-mush hours of work would be nothing without the talented, kind, generous, and outstanding authors we have encountered along the way.

This inaugural issue of something that we hope will one day be monumental to all of us involved, is dedicated to the writers.

Thank you for trusting us and thank you for ever even considering our morbid little publishing house for your work. The success experienced, will never be experienced alone.

It will always be experienced together.

Embrace the Unknown.

Questions over Innsmouth:

An Interview with Lovecraftian Scholar S.T. Joshi

(Originally published in The Gehenna Post)

Greetings from the Ether,

Almost exactly a year ago, I had the pleasure of interviewing famed Lovecraft scholar, S.T. Joshi. Perhaps the most iconic scholar of the late author, as well as an established editor and voice in the realms of weird fiction, horror, and cosmicism, it was an amazing experience and overall, humbling. For a while, we planned on releasing this interview in a newsletter. These plans fell through with the reconstruction of the publishing house, transforming from Gehenna Publishing House to what you are reading now, Gehenna & Hinnom Books. We wanted to wait for the perfect moment to release this interview, and with the site garnering so much traffic (reaching 1000+ visitors in 20 days!), we felt this was the perfect moment.

Now, I share with you the interview.

Never before seen or heard until now.

We hope you enjoy.

On World Building.

CP: Many of our readers are interested in genres like science fiction, fantasy, horror, and weird fiction, and many are authors themselves. These genres often rely on engaging and articulate world building. Authors like Tolkien are renowned for their ability to world build, but my question to you is, shouldn't Lovecraft be considered one of the greats in this field of effective world building? After all, didn't many of his works exist in the same coherent yet discrete universe?

ST: Lovecraft was absolutely one of the most accomplished "world builders" in imaginative fiction. Perhaps he doesn't get enough credit for it because, unlike Lord Dunsany, J. R. R. Tolkien, Mervyn Peake, and others, the world he built was not a realm of pure fantasy but a meticulously realised version of the objectively real world—but a real world that has been subtly distorted to accommodate the bizarre. It is clear that, in the final decade of his life, beginning with "The Call of Cthulhu" (1926), his stories use an essentially identical landscape—an imagined New England whose variegated topography (ranging from the untenanted wilderness of Vermont to the historically rich cities of Providence and Boston to fictitious towns such as Arkham and Innsmouth) and historical depth make them ideal foci for the intrusion of the weird. As a result, these stories become more than the sum of their parts, connected as they are by a complicated series of cross-references that allow them to become chapters of a long novel or saga.

On style.

CP: Lovecraft would often use colorful language and alliteration to paint canvases of horror that to this day remain unrivaled. It seems often now that such detailed styles of writing are not nearly as prevalent anymore. What are your thoughts on Lovecraft's unique style and how his style differs from current literature? Who are the Lovecrafts of today?

ST: Lovecraft, nurtured as he was on the richly textured (some would say flamboyant) prose of Edgar Allan Poe, and on later writers of dense prose such as Lord Dunsany and Arthur Machen, naturally felt that this kind of prose was ideal in creating weird atmosphere. Bizarre events are difficult to convey in austere, barebones prose, and few such authors (with the exception of M. R. James) have succeeded at it. Lovecraft was a master of prose idiom: he not only had a prodigious vocabulary, but he was supremely skilled in the ability to arrange words, sentences, and whole passages such that they convey an immensely powerful impact on the reader. It wouldn't be entirely fair to say that such dense prose has been abandoned today. Such writers as Ramsey Campbell, Caitlín R. Kiernan, and Laird Barron, while in no way imitating Lovecraft's prose, have each evolved their own distinctive styles that are anything but spare and skeletonic. Lesser-known writers such as Jonathan Thomas and Michael Aronovitz also have wondrously musical prose styles. In the specifically Lovecraftian realm, W. H. Pugmire is a luminous prose-poet whose stories and vignettes would have evoked the admiration of Lovecraft himself.

On Voice.

CP: Lovecraft's voice is one that many keen readers can detect from even a small excerpt. His concepts and language were often unrestrained and sometimes jarring. Do you believe that Lovecraft's inability to censor certain aspects of his literature was a strength or a weakness for his career? Should authors live to their own standards or is there a medium for which they should abide?

ST: It may well be the case that Lovecraft's plots and images are a bit "over-the-top" as far as the weird writing of his time is concerned; but because these plots and images are expressed in such superbly evocative prose, they are as far from being crude and amateurish as it is possible to be. Lovecraft was seeking a kind of incantatory effect in his prose, produced both by language and by incident; at times this required strong images of overt terror. But he was careful to have a proper emotional build-up to the climactic scene. In "The Call of Cthulhu," for example, the actual emergence of the entity Cthulhu at the end of the story is prepared for by a long, detailed chronicle in which we first see only an image of Cthulhu (as carved on a bas-relief), then hear about the nature of the entity through a series of interlocutors. After all this build-up, the reader is "ready" to see Cthulhu in the flesh.

On Inspiration.

CP: It is evident that Lovecraft wanted fervently to be a writer and was very passionate about bettering his skills. Many scholars have connected his mother's institutionalization and death at Butler Hospital, coupled with her emotional and psychological neglect, as precursors of influence for his unique style of writing. Do you believe that authors draw from their real-life experiences for inspiration? If so, should they? And how do you feel Lovecraft found his inspiration to write?

ST: I very much doubt that the illness of Lovecraft's mother had any direct relation to Lovecraft becoming a writer. He was an incredibly precocious boy and was already writing prose and verse at the age of six. By his early teenage years, he was writing prolifically—but his failure to graduate from high school caused him to retreat into hermitry, as he was suddenly faced with the prospect of not being able to earn a living in the profession he had chosen for himself (i.e., a professor of astronomy). Lovecraft certainly drew upon facets of his own life in his work. I believe all writers do so, but the existence of thousands of Lovecraft's letters make it transparently clear how nearly every incident in his life—as well as many of the books he read—worked their way into his creative writing, even if at times in distorted form. I don't see how writers can avoid drawing upon their own experiences—even if writing work of a weird or fantastic nature—if they wish their work to be authentic and convincing. Lovecraft had a compulsion to write weird fiction, and he felt that existing weird fiction over the previous two centuries or so had certain limitations (in imaginative scope and plausibility in the light of advances in modern science) that he sought to overcome. In this way, he evolved a new kind of weird tale that drew upon science to evoke horror not merely from conventional vampires or werewolves but from the vast cosmos beyond our sight and understanding. As such, he effected a union between weird fiction and the new genre of science fiction.

On Science Fiction.

CP: Science fiction authors are often credited for predicting future events, as the genre has classically done. Like Jules Verne with the moon, Lovecraft predicted the repercussions of what he would consider toying with cosmic forces, i.e. the Atom Bomb and the Cold War. Do you feel that the genres of science fiction offer opportunities in literary importance that other genres do not? Is it important to recognize authors like Lovecraft for these impactful predictions?

ST: I think the "predictions" of science fiction writers are oftentimes more accidental than otherwise, and I'm not sure that any *literary* value is conveyed by how accurately a given writer predicts some future event or future technological development. Science fiction, like all literature, depends for its literary quality on its ability to probe the human condition. Where Lovecraft gains his distinctiveness is in portraying in inimitable fashion the immensity of the universe and the poignancy of our insignificance and transience within that universe. That is his signature contribution to literature, and it is something he conveyed more keenly and terrifyingly than any author in literary history.

On Favorites.

CP: You have likely read everything Lovecraft has ever written. Your bibliography of Lovecraft works is the largest and most respected in the world. Of all his writing, which is your personal favorite and why?

ST: In terms of his fiction, I retain a fondness for *At the Mountains of Madness*, which I see as his greatest venture into "cosmic" fiction. The Antarctic setting is utterly convincing, and the culminating scene—where the protagonists encounter and flee from the shoggoth in the depths of the Old Ones' abandoned city—is, to my mind, the single most frightening passage in all weird fiction. Other stories such as "The Shadow over Innsmouth," "The Shadow out of Time," and "The Colour out of Space" are all immensely rich and rewarding. Some of Lovecraft's poetry—notably "The Ancient Track" and *Fungi from Yuggoth*—are quite powerful. The long essay "Supernatural Horror in Literature" is always illuminating, and other essays such as "Some Notes on a Nonentity," "Cats and Dogs," and "Some Repetitions on the Times" shed fascinating light on Lovecraft's political, social, and philosophical views.

On Future.

CP: As a scholar of Lovecraft, what are you currently working on? And what future project(s) are you most excited about?

ST: Since I have already edited corrected editions of Lovecraft's collected fiction, essays, and poetry, the only thing left for me to do is to edit Lovecraft's letters—which I am undertaking in an edition that may extend to 25 volumes or more! About 7 or 8 volumes have appeared so far from Hippocampus Press, and one or two volumes should appear every year. I'm not sure I have anything more to say about Lovecraft the man and writer, but I do want to write a little treatise about the history of Lovecraft criticism—which will really be an account of how Lovecraft emerged from the obscurity of the pulp magazines to become a world-renowned literary figure. I hope to write this work in the next year or two. And, of course, I am happy to continue compiling original anthologies of neo-Lovecraftian fiction. I have developed a fine cadre of contemporary writers who use Lovecraft as an imaginative springboard for conveying their own moods and images. I also continue to prepare editions of older weird writers, since I remain very interested in the history of weird fiction, from the dawn of literature to the present day.

Bonus Question on Current Events:

CP: On the topic of current events, what are your thoughts on the Houdini/Lovecraft drama?

ST: I presume you are referring to the discovery of three chapters of a work called *The Cancer of Superstition* that Houdini commissioned Lovecraft and his friend C. M. Eddy to ghostwrite. My initial feeling—based on statements by Eddy and August Derleth in *The Dark Brotherhood and Other Pieces* (Arkham House, 1966), where a synopsis of the book (clearly prepared by Lovecraft) and the first chapter were printed—was that the chapters were written by Eddy. But I am now thinking that Lovecraft probably had a hand in their writing, and may in fact have written them entirely. I do not think Eddy was really capable of writing these chapters, even based on raw data provided by Lovecraft. But the work as a whole is not exactly compelling and does not rank very high among Lovecraft's output.

THE SARÁYA

by Ryan Fitzpatrick

Noah stood on the edge of a gently sloping dune, the mountain path now long behind him. He put both of his hands in his pockets and smiled.

In front of him was a building. It was large and ornate and half-buried in the shifting sands of the desert. The structure pre-dated glass (he assumed), but some of the windows still featured the remnants of the original latticed woodwork, the delicate craftsmanship eroded to stubs by the near constant blasts of sand, protruding from the frames like frayed burlap or rotting teeth.

All but one of the building's four towers still featured the original, Aladdin-esque bulb at the top, and they served to adorn the structure with majesty and grandeur. A small part of him wished he knew the real architectural name for them, but a bigger part of him didn't give a shit.

Which was why he took the pictures, not wrote the articles.

He lifted his camera—a Nikon D750, the *real deal*—from his chest, and began to make his way towards the palace, firing off a few shots as he went, his legs tiring quickly as the sand sucked at his feet.

There were no people around, and in fact he had not seen anyone since he had left the small market town of Tshidi Al-Obailah over three hours ago. Weeks of research; numerous fumbling conversations with locals and government officials; countless hours spent on the internet; and sheer determination to not to let his life grind to a halt without Amy, had all led him to the dusty mountain path, which in turn, had led him here.

As he approached, the sun gave the impression of lowering itself behind the domed ceiling of the palace, creating the kind of fiery halo he had seen only in images of Christ. He took another shot.

It would be too dark to make it back to the city tonight, but he had come prepared—his pack contained two torches, a spare battery for his phone, a spare phone, a spare battery for the spare phone, a knife, thirty meters of climbing rope, a light reader, a zoom lens, three bags of nuts, two bags of trail mix, a first aid kit, two litres of drinking water, insect repellent, sun block, a change of clothes, a sleeping bag, and a tent.

He shifted the pack on his back, the weight of it acting as a constant reminder of Amy's departure. If she were here—like she *should've* been—she would have carried half as usual. But she wasn't, and the supplies jutted out of the fabric at strange angles, digging deeper into his flesh with each sinking step.

He was almost at the entrance now, the building looming high above him. He allowed himself a small smile. Life wasn't all bad, he supposed. Five big ones from the good folks at Anthropology Quarterly just for taking a few shots. Yes, *please*. Post-Islamic byzantine architecture was the theme for the day, and it was a subject as close to his heart as anything could be for a paycheck that size.

He—along with Amy—had spent weeks planning the trip, laughing together in excitement not only for the money, but the sheer adventure of it. She was a wizard when it came to the boring stuff, too: booking flights, planning connections, arranging all those meetings with guides and translators, mapping out the route, sourcing the least unpalatable (but still moderately priced) hotel, and of course, carrying half of the equipment.

He spat into the sand. She must have known even then, even as they were making plans.

But, whatever. He was here now, and the good news was that he had already done most of the hard work by finding it. This was not your standard tourist attraction with tours running eight times daily in whatever language you needed for a *very good* price. This was a *true* forgotten ruin, a building so neglected, so obliterated by the (literal) sands of time, it had never before been captured on camera. Sure, it showed up as a brown smudge on Google Earth, but that was hardly *photography*.

He was at the entrance now, and pointed the viewfinder at the cracked stonework above him. He took another shot, and entered.

It was dark inside. Much darker than he had anticipated.

He set his pack on the floor and opened the side pocket. The sound of the Velcro exploded into the silence, and he winced in response.

From the pack, he pulled a Maglite, switching it on and pointing it into the darkness. He shook it, the batteries rattling back at him as they echoed from the surface of unseen shapes. The beam did not improve, and he realised that the problem was not the torch, but his eyes— they had not yet adjusted to the gloom. He reached back into the pack and pulled out the light meter instead, aiming it into the shadows.

F3.07. Not bad. Perfectly workable with a wide aperture and a high ISO.

He stood inert, waiting for his eyes to adjust.

As they did, the entranceway began to take shape around him. Each wall featured a mosaic of tiny, coloured tiles, creating broken isometric patterns stretching far up into the central column above him. Below, the floor was a mixture of stone, plaster, and fallen tiles, which lay strewn across the windblown ridges of sand throughout. He shuffled his foot from side to side, but could not see the building's true topography.

Lifting the camera, he framed his first interior shot. It showed the staircase before him, curving upwards and then back in on itself, splitting into two luxurious arcs and disappearing high above his head and out of shot.

He pressed the button, heard the shutter fall, and tilted the camera to see the 3 x 4.5-inch display.

It was okay, but it wouldn't win him the Pulitzer. He turned one-eighty and framed the desert between the grand stone arches instead.

There was a *thud* from somewhere above him. His muscles tightened and he froze, his finger poised above the Big Black Button.

One of the things he learnt from his work for Derelict—a magazine covering exactly what you'd expect from the title—was that abandoned places never stayed that way for long, and he still remembered the day he had slowly backed out of a room in which he had found a homeless man masturbating.

That was the kind of thing you didn't forget.

No follow-up sound came, and he brought the lens back up to his face with a sigh. This was the middle of the desert, not the inner city, and judging by the amount of crap surrounding him, it was probably just another chunk of plaster coming loose, giving up its place on the wall for a new life on the floor.

He adjusted the focus through the viewfinder with a trembling hand, re-framing the shot and pressing the button. He looked at the results.

Not bad.

He took a deep breath, steadying nerves that he would not admit had been un-steadied, and began to explore.

Fifteen minutes later, and he was back at the bottom of the stairs.

He had spent the time doing a lap of the ground floor, bringing the shutter down on anything that might interest the folks at Anthropology Quarterly. From his limited experience, they especially seemed to like the little things—the way a window was clasped; the construction of walls; closeups of any ornaments or vases. And, with a hundred and twenty-eight gigabytes of storage on his camera—and another sixty-four on a memory card in his pack—he did not need to be frugal.

But he *did* need to hurry up. He took out his phone.

After quickly scrolling through hundreds of pictures of Amy in various stages of undress, he found what he was looking for: the screenshot of the website he had taken before leaving. It told him that the sun would set in or around the next thirty minutes or so, and that gave him just enough time to give the second floor a quick glance to see what he was working with tomorrow.

He slipped the phone back into his pocket and began to move up the stairs, testing each one with the press of a toe before transferring his weight. They seemed stable enough, and he continued to move up them, running his arm along the curve of the wall as he went.

At the top, the tattered fragments of a rug hung listlessly over the first few steps, and as he approached them, saw that the carpet stretched all the way to the far side of the building, the tiled floor visible through its holes.

He stood in what was clearly the central corridor. From it, several rooms branched off, dusky sunlight the colour of fire streaming through each of the arched doorways, casting shapes onto the rug, like inverse shadows.

It was beautiful, and Noah took his opportunity.
Click.

He titled the screen once more, and, pleased he had taken his first award-winning photo of the trip—he usually took around thirty that he believed truly deserved accolade, something that the people at *Hotten & Holder* had so far failed to recognize—he moved into the first room.

It was decorated with the same ornate tiling as the entrance hall, and was larger than his entire flat back home. Through the windows, he saw that the sun was little more than a slither of light resting on the top of the mountains.

Not a bad place for a final cigarette before setting up for the night.

He lifted himself onto the ledge of the open window and let his legs dangle towards the sand. The sun grew smaller as he watched, and he pulled out an already battered cigarette carton, lighting one up and inhaling deep.

The air was cooler now, and the money for the shoot was pretty much in the bag. He felt good. Free. The best part was, he wasn't thinking of Amy. Not one bit.

Which was good. Because she'd ditched him. Moved half way across the country. And for what?

A pointless degree in Computer Sciences, that's what.

She must have known. She must have known.

The thought played itself on a loop over and over in his mind, a bad mantra for a bad situation. Getting into college—especially at thirty-two—takes time, and she must have applied long before she had ever broached the subject with him.

Maybe she was trying to spare his feelings.

If so, it didn't work, because the worst part of all of this, the most gut-wrenching and soul-destroying *bitch* of the whole situation, was that she must have known. She must have *known* and kept planning anyway, letting him believe that she wasn't about to dump his ass and leave him with an apartment he couldn't afford on his own, a group of friends he never much liked in the first place, and a housecat that, quite frankly, he hated a little more with each passing day without her.

He took another drag of the cigarette, letting it rip at his throat.

Well, fuck Amy. What did she care anyway; she was probably blowing some guy in her dorm room just for the goddamn fun of it. The *college experience,* she called it.

His emotional pain manifested itself in his fingers, and he looked down to see that the cigarette was nothing more than an orange stub pinched between two smouldering fingers. He flicked the butt up into the air and shook out his hand, watching the ember perform a dancing arc across the night sky.

Amy wouldn't've approved, but fuck it. Anyway, what harm would one more cigarette butt do in a world where turtles choked to death on beer can wrappers?

He sighed and took one last look out at the mountains. The sun was nothing more than a glow behind them, and he looked back into the room to see that it was black. The archway he had entered through had disappeared into the darkness, and he could no longer see where the debris on the floor lay.

Stupid. What did he *think* was going to happen if he watched the sunset? Goddamn it.

He swung his legs back over the ledge, catching his calf on something sharp in the process.

"Shit," he whispered, hopping from the ledge onto his good foot and lifting his damaged one to look at it.

Whatever was on the ledge had sliced through the material of his pants and cut a deep groove into the meat of his leg. The wound was painful and was already bleeding, the warm wetness running down his calf and gathering in his sock. He held the cloth of his pants against it for a few moments, waiting for it to congeal.

The pain was getting worse, and his pant leg was now fully damp with blood. He stood, pondering the benefits of travel insurance, wondering exactly what the benefits were if you're bleeding to death in the desert, and then straightened out suddenly. If he didn't get going soon, he might be stuck here for the night, and although he'd been considering it earlier, the sudden darkness combined with the loud noise above him had made the tent sound much more appealing.

Before he could do anything, he needed light, and with a horrible sinking feeling in his stomach, realised he couldn't remember where he had left his pack. Was it at the top of the stairs or somewhere in here?

Shit.

From somewhere in the darkness of the corridor, there was another sound. It was unlike the thudding from before, but had the same effect. He felt the hair on his exposed neck rise.

He waited.

This time, no dust motes were visible dancing in the light, and in fact, Noah couldn't see *anything.* He lifted his foot gently and placed it a few centimetres in front of him.

The sound came again, and once more, he froze. It was a soft patting noise, like fingertips tapping cardboard.

He lifted his other foot slowly, bringing it in line with the first one. When he placed it down, he gritted his teeth together, already forgetting how bad the pain in his leg was.

Pat ... pat ... pat ...

Stepping further into the darkness with his arms outstretched, he suddenly felt the cool firmness of the doorway.

Pat ... pat ... pat ...

Closer now. He would check the landing for his pack first, try to avoid doubling back on himself if he didn't need too.

Passing through the arch, he slowly bent down and began running his hands over the floor, caressing the ragged and sand-swept carpet in search of his bag.

A shuffle from behind him. This time, it was the sound of a cadaver dragging a twisted foot along the smooth tiled floor beside the carpet.

He closed his eyes against the image and began to move his hands quicker. Where the fuck was this god-damn pack?

The sound came again. It was still light, almost unperceivable, but it was *there*. Whoever or whatever it was, was close now, and did not want him to know about it. There was a smell now too, familiar yet ugly. He was about to make a run for it, pack or no pack, when he lay his hands on the blessedly familiar touch of fabric.

Got it.

He undid the flap and groped for his light, the noise of his fumbling sounding uncomfortably loud in the isolation. His fingers touched metal, and he swung the pack over his shoulder, whipping the torch out of the pocket and switching it on.

In front of him were three sets of eyes, so blindingly bright in reflection that they obscured whatever creature—or creatures—they belonged too. Two of the pairs were high above his head, and seemed to be looking down on him.

He dropped the torch and ran.

He was in darkness again, but enough of the torch light reflected from the walls of the space to illuminate the stairs beneath him as he took them two at a time, gliding his arm along the wall as a guide.

Behind him, he could hear the unseen creatures give chase.

He kept the pace up, each step causing his leg to scream out in agony, his mind searching through the hundreds of hours he had spent watching those Attenborough documentaries with Amy and trying to recall an animal that tall that could possibly be in the desert.

He came up blank. But it didn't matter. He was on the ground floor again now, bolting towards the small portion of night sky that signified the doorway. He made it through, but kept running anyway, the large and angular pack digging into his back with each frantic step.

A sudden dip in the sand caused him to lose his footing and fall. His face connected with the sand.

After a moment's dizziness, he sat up suddenly, digging his backup torch from his pack and directing it into the gloom of the building.

Three domestic-sized cats were circling the entrance.

Their fur was mangy, and one of them was missing an ear. All three stood looking at him, not seeming to want to come any farther into the sand. They circled the doorway for a few more seconds and then retreated into the darkness.

Cats!

Noah spat out the sand and threw his head back to the stars. He laughed, long and deep and uncontrollably, until tears formed in the corners of his eyes. For the first time since he had arrived, he was glad Amy was not there.

It was morning again, and the sun illuminated the walls of his tent, making them glow ethereal around him. He wriggled out of his sleeping bag, his body already clammy in the morning heat.

He pulled out a cigarette and tried to light it up, but the sand had infected the gears of his lighter when he fell, and the wheel grounded to a dissatisfying halt. He threw it into the corner of the tent and pulled out a box of matches instead, striking one against the strip. He lit the cigarette and inhaled. The warm air of the tent made it taste stale and unpleasant, and he only smoked it to about halfway before opening the flap and stubbing it into the sand.

He sat this way for a while, letting the sun beat down on his naked legs, careful to keep his wound from going the same way as the lighter.

Last night, even after his embarrassing feline revelation, the experience of the chase had still unsettled him, the panic of the moment leaving a coppery taste in the back of his throat.

The abandoned palace had loomed large in his dreams, too; encounters with Lovecraftian horrors tainting his subconscious. It was stupid, sure, but even in the light of day, the building was somehow ominous, eternal, a solitary rebellion against the desolate landscape that surrounded it.

That's good, he thought with a grimace, *I'll use that in my acceptance speech.*

It was a sour thought.

Well, whatever. He was here now, and he had a job to do. Five grand went a long way towards the grocery list, especially when it was just for one.

He pulled out his phone and checked the time. His taxi would be picking him up for his return flight at four, and the trail back to the city took at least three hours, which, all in all, left him with two hours to pack away, get his photos, and get the hell out of dodge.

Which was fine. The sooner he was out of here, the better.

He began to pack.

For the second time, he crossed the threshold and waited for his eyes to adjust.

The entrance was the same as he had seen it yesterday, albeit slightly brighter. There were no cats in sight, which was just fine by him. He re-took a few of the shots he had taken last night—now in better lighting—and then ascended the stairs, passing by where he had watched the sunset.

Along the top of the hallway, lining both sides, was a ridge just about wide enough for a cat. He shook his head and continued.

As he moved through the rooms, he became aware of the trail the feral cats had left, and wondered just how many were living here. Droppings lined most of the corridors, and increased in quantity each time he moved up a floor. They were accompanied by an increasingly unpleasant smell, and although he hadn't seen any cats since last night, they were obviously still here. Sometimes, he could even hear them moving through the walls.

By the time he reached the fourth floor, his T-shirt was sticky with sweat, and he smelled almost as bad as his surroundings. He considered pulling the spare out of the pack, but decided to push on instead.

He lifted the camera, framing a window and the desert beyond.

He heard a soft *thud* behind him and turned.

It was one of the cats, a different one from the three he had seen last night. This one was missing an eye, a pale fluid oozing from the socket where it had been. On its body, only a few barest patches of fur were present, making its grey skin visible beneath. Noah took a step back.

The animal stood and looked at him with its head to one side, and then took a casual step towards him.

"*Shoo*," he whispered, waving his arm as if brushing dust from a table.

The creature flinched, paused, and then continued. Noah took another step backwards, holding his camera like a shield.

It ignored his flailing arm and approached him, extending its neck and trying to nuzzle his bad leg. He pushed it away gently with his foot.

It began to walk back towards him almost immediately.

He gave up and turned back to the window, letting the animal perform figures of eight between his legs. Great; now he'd have to check his vaccination book when he got back, see what was overdue. Probably have to get Larry sorted too, lest the stupid animal caught anything he brought back on his clothes.

He brought the viewfinder up to his eye and pressed the button, hearing the familiar and satisfying *click*. At the same moment, he felt a rough tongue lick his wound through the gash in his cargo pants.

He dropped the camera so suddenly that it swung on its strap and smashed against his solar plexus, knocking the air out of him. He looked down to see the cat grinning up at him and licking its lips.

In a moment of reactive horror—his motor neuron functions bypassing his brain completely—he kicked out with his foot, connecting with the animal's ribcage and sending it in a low arc through the air. Its legs scrambled as it flew, and it landed with a *thud*, hissing at him before scampering away.

He stood for a few seconds in disbelief, half for the cats behaviour and half for his own. No matter what happened on this trip, he could never tell *anyone* that he had kicked a cat. That kind of thing just didn't look good on your resume. He shook his head.

"This place is *fucked*," he mumbled.

Just one more floor and he could get out of here.

The final stairway was shaped like a spiral, with a high-sided balustrade following the curve. Here, even more faeces lined the walls. Most were in the form of hardened lumps that buzzed with flies, but every now and again he would see one that was more like liquid, sprayed in obscene arcs across the wall.

He brought his T-shirt up to his face and followed the staircase, trying to take shallow breaths. The smell was getting worse, and it was darker here too. He turned on the flash and fired off a few more shots. These kind of photographs—basically graphic images of faeces—were obviously not part of his assignment, but if *Anthropology Quarterly* wasn't interested in a community of feral animals living in the desert, *someone* out there would be. It could even be his masterpiece . . .

At the top of the stairs, he stopped.

This floor was not like the others.

Instead of being separated into smaller, more domestic-size spaces, it had been left open, spanning the entire length of the building. It's domed ceiling and elaborate tiling made the grand entranceway look meek by comparison. The morning light poured into the space like condensed electricity, and at the very far side was the faded and lopsided remains of a throne.

But none of this is what caught Noah's attention. Noah was looking at the pit.

It formed the centrepiece of the room, and was about half the size of a swimming pool. It was overflowing with the bones of animals, stripped clean of all but the grizzliest flesh and cartilage.

Surrounding it, were the cats.

Hundreds of them.

Most lay together in groups, basking in the sun, their bodies moulding themselves into the shape of the light from the windows. Others walked lazily across the room, stopping only to gnaw on unidentifiable hunks of flesh from the pit.

The aroma was unbearable, and in a few places, he could make out the near-liquid corpses of dead cats as they lay rotting in the heat, the sickly-sweet smell of their decomposition clinging to the inside of his throat like honey, despite the T-shirt.

Next to him, stretching all the way to the far wall, lay what he could only describe as a pile of cats. Fat, hairless babies mewled and sucked at their mother's teat, their bodies—easily in the hundreds—overlapping until the whole thing looked like one disgusting alien organism, pink and hairy and matted with the offal of birth. The creature pulsated in waves and breathed as one. He suppressed a gag and looked back in the direction of the pit. Behind it, right at the back of the room, on the remnants of the throne, three cats were trying to fornicate with each other at the same time.

Noah stood in the doorway and took it all in. It was creepy. It was bizarre. It was absolutely fucking satanic. He lifted the camera to his face and framed the shot.

This could be the one.

As the shutter fell, the flash from the end of his camera exploded, sending dazzling white light into the far reaches of the room.

Five-hundred pairs of eyes turned to see the intruder. He froze.

What now?

That's when they began to move.

It was slow at first, their heads and eyes continuing to stare as their bodies rose. It was as if they were synchronised, all the animals moving, no, *hunting*, as one.

The mass rising was slow enough for a cartoon image to come to his mind; he would back out of the room with his hands up saying *nice kitty . . .*

They began to move faster, a few chosen leaders seeming to set the pace for the others. Noah could only stare at them, struck by the absurdity of his situation. Was he about to run from a group of cats that were no larger than Larry, who was probably sitting in his apartment right now, happily munching on a dish of cat-food laid out by Mrs. Krasnik from Flat 308?

Quite possibly.

The red mouths within the fleshy pink thing began to wail, as if sensing their broken sanctuary. It was a high-pitched sound, and the volume of their combined mewling was deafening. Noah put his hands against his ears. The movement was sudden, and the other cats took this as their signal, beginning to charge towards him proper, their yellow teeth bared in anger.

Or hunger.

Noah did not stay to find out which it was. He turned and bolted down the stairs.

He was almost halfway around the first spiral when he felt a weight hit the back of his pack. The sudden force made him miss the next few steps, and he tripped, regaining his balance with the help of the balustrade and ignoring the pain in his leg. He was pretty sure it was bleeding again, but was too busy trying to shake off the creature on his pack to care.

Three white hot scalpels pierced the flesh on the back of his neck, gouging at him. He screamed out in pain and threw the bag over his left shoulder, catching it on his right. The animal came with it, but so did a large portion of his neck. He had just enough time to see the red and white chunk, still attached to the animal's claws, as he swung the pack into the nearest wall. He heard a crunch of bone and was hit with a gust of rotting meat as the breath was expelled from the animal. It dropped from the pack.

He kept moving. Behind him, he could hear them getting closer.

The blood was hot and wet on his back, but he ignored it.

He turned in time to see another cat sail through the air, it's claws drawn, its whiskers taut, and its eyes alive with hunger. He sidestepped it, and watched as it cleared another ten steps, landing awkwardly on the ledge below him. It was apparently un-phased, and tried to leap again as he passed. This time, he saw it coming, and kicked.

"Fuck *you!*" he shouted as his foot connected with its head. It soared through the air again, this time its body spinning gracelessly and its legs splayed out limply. At the bottom, he passed it for a second time—its head at an impossible angle halfway up the first step—but hardly looked at it.

As he ran, his head was filled with the images of the decaying animals he had seen upstairs. The pit. The birthing creature. The claw marks on the drapes. What was going on here? A rabies outbreak of some kind, maybe? Cats just didn't behave like that normally, did they?

It didn't matter. The only important thing was that they would not follow him out onto the sand; not if last night was anything to go by.

He continued to run, all the way across the hallway and then down the next flight of steps, the camera beating against his chest as it swung from his neck and the pack digging further into his back. His leg felt weak, too, and he began to slow.

He risked a look back, and saw that they were no longer in pursuit. There was not a sign of fur in sight, and the sounds were now distant.

He stopped, resting his hands on his knees and leaning on the wall. Around him, the air once again danced with dust motes, and he watched as each ragged breath sent them scattering.

He considered pulling the water from his pack—god knows he needed it—but decided to push on instead. The sooner he was out of here and on his way to a doctor, the better.

The next three floors passed without incident. He could still hear the cats as they moved, but their wailing and shuffling was still distant. His progress was slow now, and his neck was on fire.

In front of him was a long corridor, the final one before the stairs to the main entrance. He began to walk down it, using the wall to steady himself, again wondering what kinds of diseases lay under the claws of a feral cat.

This wouldn't have happened if Amy was here, he thought, his foot dragging beside him as he inched down the impossibly long corridor, the same image he had pictured the night before. In a way, it was her fault. If she was here, she would never have let things get this far. He may not have listened to her at first, obviously, but eventually . . .

A noise, closer now.

He took another step and then stopped.

From around the corner came a stampede of slender hairy bodies. They raced towards him, their ranks as wide as the corridor would allow, leaping and clawing and hissing and weaving, clamouring over each other to get to him first. On the ledges around the top of the corridor, the animals charged in single file. He watched with dumb disbelief as one of them fell, disappearing into the undulating sea of matted fur as it coursed towards him.

Ambushed, he thought. *What the fuck?*

There was no other way down but through them.

Spreading his legs a little, he slid the travel pack off his shoulder and held it like a weapon, both straps firmly clasped in the super strength grip of adrenaline.

He began to run towards them, swinging the bag like a golf club.

He hit the first three cats dead on, sending them scattering amongst the others. He continued running, feeling the crunch of a tiny ribcage beneath his feet, lifting the pack high above his head for another swing.

As he did so, an animal with long, dust-coloured hair latched onto his thigh, sinking it's claws into his flesh. It hung from the perforations in his flesh, and he brought the pack down on it. Just before impact, he saw that the bag had picked up a passenger from the ridge above, and the two cats hit each other back to back, their eyeballs bulging and their bones contorting. They both fell.

He was halfway to the stairs now, and ducked to avoid four sets of barbed paws as one of the animals leapt from the upper ridge. It sailed above his head, but he did not stop to see where it landed.

They were getting more frantic now, becoming aware, maybe, that their dinner was about to escape out of the front door.

He felt an intense and sudden pain in his left ankle, and looked down to see one of the animals with its teeth sunk as far as his bone. He kicked out, but it hung onto him the way he had seen lions hang onto antelope in those nature documentaries. He felt the skin rip and screamed out in agony.

They were all over him now, and he was still trying to kick the one on his ankle off when three more white hot balls of pain erupted across his body. He looked down to see a cat that had its teeth deep into his right forearm. He grabbed at its head and lifted it out of his flesh, blood beginning to flow from the two holes in his skin. He threw it into the wall and kept moving.

Somewhere, deep beneath the pain, panic, and adrenaline, he realised he had made it to the top of the stairs.

He began to descend, and as he did so, they leapt from the higher ground, latching onto his exposed flesh with claw and fang. He screamed out in agony and bent over suddenly, throwing several of the cats from his skin.

He tried to swing the pack again, but it had become too heavy to lift, and he dropped it. He felt a sudden warmth on his neck as one of the cats clawed at the still-fresh wound that lay there.

The cats were all over him again now, and the next thing he saw were three, dirty pearl-coloured claws, lashing out towards his eyes. The paw reached its target, raking across his forehead and right eye, making him feel as if his face was being pressed into a bed of nails.

He lifted his arms involuntarily, but the weight of the cats that hung from them made it too much, too heavy, and all he succeeded in doing was widening the lacerations.

He felt a furry wetness on his face and clamped his teeth down instinctively. His mouth was suddenly filled with hot coppery liquid, and he spat out a chunk of warm wet flesh. Through a blinking, blood-filled left eye, he saw that it was a cat's snout, the little pink nose still twitching in the sand. The rest of the creature fell from his chest, the gap in the middle of its face filling with thick black liquid.

He was at the bottom of the stairs now, and a shaft of brilliant, golden light filled the entrance, a luminous path to the desert beyond.

He took a step forward and fell, feeling more bones crunch beneath him.

Within seconds, the rest of the brood were on him.

He tried to fight back, but the fight had left.

He fell forwards into a bed of matted fur, feeling the animals underneath him claw and scratch at his chest and groin as they tried to escape from the combined weight above them. His stomach tore and he heard the contents spill into the sand below.

He experienced his final thought in darkness. It was one word, and did nothing to comfort him.

Amy.

Ryan Fitzpatrick lives and writes in the UK. The Sarāya is his second published work.

WAX SOLDIERS

by Kurt Newton

The landscape was a maze of abandoned buildings and cobblestone alleyways. Heaps of rubble forced Simms to navigate through a crumbling tenement in the hope of reaching his checkpoint. He had become separated from his unit, but it wasn't the first time he had found himself in enemy territory outnumbered and outgunned.

Simms climbed through a blast hole in the building's south wall and stepped into another narrow alleyway. The alley brought him to the edge of a courtyard. He stopped to listen for the march of foot soldiers, and was about to break into the open when he heard a tumble of brick from behind. He wheeled, gun raised. It was one of them—tall, thin, dressed in black body armor, black boots, black face shield. The face shield was contoured to mimic human features, yet designed to render them featureless, uniform, indistinguishable from each other.

Simms shot, his reflexes responding to the sudden threat. The soldier landed in a sitting position against the rubble, the bullet piercing the combatant's faceplate. Simms walked over and lifted the mask. The face beneath was just as featureless. As Simms examined the soldier for intel, the head wound began to close. Soon, there would be nothing of the wound but a small circular blemish. Simms didn't wait around. The gunshot had drawn attention.

He scrambled out into the open and ducked behind a debris pile: the remains of what was once a church. A stone cross jutted from the pile like the mast of a sunken ship. Pieces of stained glass littered the ground.

Three soldiers marched into view.

Simms checked his gun clip. Only one round left. It could have been a hundred for all it mattered. He had shot at them before. The bullets tugged at their uniform but they just kept coming.

Simms surveyed his surroundings. There was an abandoned truck ten yards away, its engine compartment destroyed by a grenade, however its gas tank appeared intact. Simms hoped this to be so. It was his last chance. He waited for the soldiers to pass near the truck, took aim and fired.

The truck lifted off the ground, exploding in a fireball. The soldiers lay lifeless beneath a rain of shrapnel. Simms should have run, but instead he approached the burning wreck and the bodies that lay beside it. Each of the soldiers had been burned by the blast—uniform charred and smoldering, face gone, wiped clean by the flames.

Simms worked quickly, collecting weapons and ammo. When the heat became unbearable, he stepped back, but it wasn't soon enough. His hand began to drip, the skin sloughing off. He stepped back further and the dripping slowed, then stopped altogether. Almost immediately, the damaged skin began to regenerate, filling in the portions he had lost.

By now, the enemy soldiers were nearly unrecognizable as men, just clothing resting atop puddles of liquid slag. But Simms knew, once the truck had burned itself out, they too would return to what they were. It was the way of war; it was never-ending.

Simms looked toward the sky to check the position of the sun. He then chose a direction and fled before more soldiers arrived.

Simms reached his checkpoint by sundown rejuvenated, ready for the next battle.

Kurt Newton's dark fiction has appeared in *Weird Tales*, *Weirdbook*, *Dark Discoveries*, and *Shroud*. He is the author of two novels, *The Wishnik* and *Powerlines*. He is a lifelong resident of the Connecticut woods.

BEQUEATH

by G.A. Miller

3:02 AM

Mark Baker gasped loudly, waking from the nightmare. The same nightmare that haunted him since *it* happened, so long ago.

He was in the shower after gym class, his eyes closed as he washed his hair, trying to prevent the shampoo from getting into his eyes and stinging them.

Suddenly, he was pushed hard from behind, the force causing him to slip and fall on the wet tiles. He rubbed his eyes with his fingers, opening them to see a circle of wet feet surrounding him.

The first stream of hot urine hit his face, causing him to gag and squeeze his eyes closed as the other streams began, all aiming for his head, his face. He opened his mouth to cry for help, and one of them scored a bullseye, right in his mouth. He retched and gagged, vomiting on the floor, as they all laughed while emptying their bladders.

In his nightmare, those bladders never seemed to empty, their urine hot enough to burn his skin. Then, the cleansing water from the shower heads all turned into forceful yellow jets of boiling hot urine, his skin blistering as he flailed helplessly on the floor before them.

He sat up, tears running down his face, and went into the bathroom, ashamed that he now had to empty his own bladder.

Monday had arrived.

Mark Baker wasn't the sort of man to stand out in a crowd. Slender build, average height and coloring. No distinct features to speak of, he naturally blended into the background of any surrounding.

He lived quietly, renting a small apartment for himself, working as a bookkeeper in a large company, just another faceless occupant in a cubicle. He had no close friends, never really did, having been the preferred target of every bully in every school he'd ever attended.

That harsh childhood taught him to keep quiet, to look down, and try not to be noticed—traits he'd kept as an adult. It also fueled a very deep-seated hatred for the world in general, which he wasn't even consciously aware of, having accepted his fate long ago.

The last time he'd tried to become friendly with one of his co-workers, he later overheard her talking to a friend, describing Mark as "having the personality of an orphaned sock." A bright flare of anger briefly burned inside him, but then he silently sat in his cubicle, blushing furiously, waiting until she'd left the office before gathering his things to go home. He understood he simply didn't know how to socialize, never having had the chance to learn when he was growing up.

But understanding didn't lessen the pain and embarrassment.

He caught the 5:17 bus, as he usually did, and had a window seat. He opened the newspaper in his lap, but gazed out the window instead, watching the world pass by, wondering what it was like to be different, to be confident, like the men standing outside their homes talking and laughing as they collected the mail from the boxes at the curb. There were probably wives inside those houses, maybe children too, waiting for Daddy to walk in, excited and happy to see him arrive.

Folding his paper, he stood and pulled the signal cord, his stop approaching soon. He exited the bus and walked to his apartment building, glancing at the mail boxes in the vestibule wall. Was that an envelope? He wasn't expecting any utility bills for at least another week or two. He opened his box to find a lone envelope addressed to him from "Quimby and Howe, Solicitors," with a return address in London. He locked his mail box and went inside, taking the stairs up to his small apartment on the second floor.

He set his things down absently, wondering if he'd received the letter by mistake. He opened it with a butter knife, and sat down at the small kitchenette table to read.

It said his grandfather had a brother named Edgar who'd settled in England after World War One, spent the rest of his life there, and had left behind one item that he bequeathed to the last living male member of their family, which happened to be Mark. They apologized profusely for the long delay in locating him, finally succeeding by using the new ancestry databases that had become so popular. They'd enclosed a legal release form and a self-addressed, stamped envelope for its return, asking him to please sign and date and then return it to them at his earliest convenience.

Upon receipt of the release, they'd ship the item from his grand uncle directly to him, and would consider the matter properly closed.

Mark was stunned. He now remembered family members occasionally referring to someone "over there," but they were immediately hushed by the others, as though speaking of a secret meant to be kept hidden, a black sheep of some kind. His parents never spoke about him to Mark, and he'd completely forgotten about it until now.

He wondered what this item was—as they'd only referred to it as an item—with no further description. He was positive it wouldn't be anything of value, though. Things like that simply don't happen to him, and this would be no different. Probably a souvenir from the war, or something like that. He signed and dated the release form, folded it into the return envelope, and left it on the table next to his keys, so he'd remember to mail it in the morning.

Weeks passed, and Mark had forgotten about the letter. He arrived home one Friday to find a folded piece of paper in the grate of his mail box. He removed it, and found a note from George, the building superintendent, asking him to stop by when he got home. He walked down the hall to George's apartment, hoping a pipe hadn't burst, or some other disaster, and rang the bell.

"Hello, George . . . you wanted to see me?"

"Hi, Mr. Baker, yes. A package came for you today; they let me sign for it. One minute," he stepped over to a table in his hallway, reaching for something there.

"Here you go," George returned, handing Mark a small cardboard box with labels all over it.

"Thank you, George. I appreciate you signing for it for me."

"No problem, Mr. Baker. You have a good one now." Smiling, George closed his door as Mark examined the box. He turned it over and saw his name and address, with "Quimby and Howe, Solicitors," as the return address.

So, this was the mysterious item they'd mailed him about. He went upstairs to his apartment, put it aside, and set about making his supper.

Once the dinner dishes were cleaned and put away, Mark sat down and used a pair of scissors to cut the tape securing the box and opened it. Inside was a folded letter, and a small wooden box, once polished to a high gloss, but marred heavily with dents and tool marks. He opened the letter, which apologized for the deplorable condition of the box, stating that this was how it came into their possession, clearly from failed attempts to pry it open.

They ascertained what appeared to be a seam, indicating that it *should* open, but were unable to determine *how* to open it. As such, they encouraged him to report any valuables he might find inside to the appropriate authorities for tax purposes, and wished him well.

He set the letter aside, and picked up the box. He turned it over, feeling weight inside it, but seeing no obvious way to unlock it. The deep gouges in it showed many attempts at forcing it open, which hadn't seemed to work. He held it in both hands, and smiled, remembering an old cartoon he'd watched.

"Open Sesame..." he whispered, using his thumbs to push up on the top half of the box.

It opened smoothly and easily on hidden hinges.

He was so startled, he nearly dropped it. In the bottom, set in a cushion of black satin, was a ring. It was gold, but a darker shade of the yellow than he'd ever seen in gold jewelry, with a deep blue gemstone speckled with gilded dots, resembling stars in the night sky. Toward the bottom, the dots changed to red, and finally to black at the very edge. The sides of the ring surrounding the stone were engraved with what appeared to be dragons reaching toward the center. It looked like it had been made by hand, not nearly as refined as the rings you might see in a modern display case.

In the top of the case, there was a rolled-up parchment with a black ribbon around it. He removed it, and revealed words etched by hand into the wood itself, *"Daemonium Et Dimittere,"* whatever that meant. Maybe the ring makers?

He carefully opened the parchment and found one lone sentence and a symbol, both clearly written by hand. The sentence simply said, *"Do What Thou Wilt,"* and under that, a symbol with a five petaled flower at the center of a diamond shape, with wings of some sort stretching out to each side:

Mark was thoroughly confused. He'd originally thought the ring had something to do with his great uncle's military background, perhaps a symbol adopted by his battalion, but the parchment and ring design didn't look to be military at all. He carefully rolled the old parchment back up, sliding it back into the black ribbon, and setting it inside the cover of the box. He put the box down on the table, leaving it open. He had a feeling it wouldn't open for him so easily again if he closed it.

"Oh, Uncle Edgar, what the hell were you mixed up with?" he wondered aloud. He looked over at the ring, but never actually touched it. Something about the signet made him a little uneasy, but he couldn't say what or why. He decided to do some research and see what he could find out.

He opened his small Chromebook, hoping Ross had a signal available upstairs. His neighbor Ross allowed Mark to piggyback on his wireless signal in exchange for a few dollars a month against the cost, a deal that worked well for them both. It connected perfectly, and be began searching for more information about the puzzling box and its contents.

An hour later, the notepad beside his Chromebook was full of notes he'd taken, most very disturbing. He wondered how deep into insanity his grand uncle had fallen when he put the box and its contents together.

The phrase etched into the top of the box turned out to be Latin for "Release the Demon." As bad as that was, the phrase on the parchment, "Do What Thou Wilt," was attributed to an Aleister Crowley: a notorious medium and rumored Satanist in England, at about the time his grand uncle had settled there after the war. He found endless references to Crowley, none very flattering, and finally learned that the stone in the ring appeared to be a

Lapis Lazuli, rumored to enhance communication with spirits, among other things. He surmised his uncle had met and become a disciple of Crowley's, based on the layout of the box and its contents.

So, he'd received a ring, somehow connected with a very bad man, seemingly for the purpose of releasing a demon of some kind.

In other words, this was all nonsense, the sort of thing that kids tell each other around campfires to scare themselves. He wondered if his grand uncle had come back with severe PTSD, long before it had been recognized, and that led him to this Crowley individual, who clearly preyed on weak-minded followers in his cult, or whatever his following was.

Relieved, and now more curious, Mark lifted the ring out of the cushion in the box. He was surprised at its weight, heavier than he'd expected. The only marking inside the band was the single word, *"Asmodeus,"* but he had a feeling that the gold was real. At this weight, he just might have something of value to declare, after all.

It was large too, clearly made for a bigger hand than his. For the fun of it, he slipped it onto the index finger of his right hand, and found that it fit perfectly, as if it were made for him.

He held up his hand to look at it, and felt a little lightheaded for a moment. He'd never owned or worn any jewelry at all, but didn't think the skin contact with the gold would cause the odd feeling. As he turned his hand to look from all angles, he realized he felt a surge of confidence, something he wasn't used to at all.

Along with that, there was a feeling of contempt for himself, for allowing himself to be victimized time and time again, simply accepting his fate as though he had no choice. His renewed sense of confidence seemed to assure him that those days were over forever.

He started to remove the ring and put it back in the box, but stopped. He *enjoyed* the sensations he was feeling, and if they were somehow related to the ring, then why remove it? He closed his right hand slowly into a fist and smiled. Remembering the inscription inside the band, he returned to his Chromebook, and quickly learned that 'Asmodeus' was one of the seven princes of hell, known for lust, and as a revenger of wickedness.

His smile widened as he realized how useful those two particular attributes could prove to be . . .

7:46 AM

Mark Baker opened his eyes slowly, adjusting to the brightness in the room, and realized two things.

He was smiling happily, this time from the new dream he'd just had, and he'd also awakened with a painful erection that had nothing to do with bladder control.

He needed a woman, and he meant to have one. Soon.

His new dream had begun the same as before, in the shower after gym class, his eyes closed as he washed his hair, trying to prevent the shampoo from getting in his eyes and stinging them.

This time, however, when the push came, he was ready for it, and spun around quickly to face Chuck Richardson, the captain of the football team, and his tormentor-in-chief.

"What the fuck is your problem, Richardson?"

"Well, what do we have here?" Chuck laughed, "it seems the worm is growing a set of balls!"

He and his friends all laughed, as Chuck moved in closer

"Lemmie show you what it means to have balls, wimp."

As Chuck reached out to grab him, Mark turned to his left and reached up between the outstretched arms, grabbing Chuck by the throat. With more force than he could account for, he easily spun Chuck around and slammed him back into the tile wall, hard enough to break a few of the tiles.

"Hey, leave him alone, Baker!" one of his friends yelled, but Mark paid no mind. He stared instead at Chuck as his grip tightened. He didn't even notice that his hand had grown larger, the fingernails extending out to thick, sharp points.

"No, peasant, the worm has turned, and your time has come . . ." Mark's voice had changed, dropping much deeper in timbre, very rough and raspy. Chuck's friends started to step back, unsure of what was happening.

Mark's thick nails allowed him to press in on either side of Chuck's throat, tearing through the skin, letting him wrap his fist around the jugular itself. The sheeting blood splattered the floor, turning red instead of yellow in this version of the dream.

Chuck's friends started running for the open door, a few screaming as they escaped. Only one or two looked back in time to see Mark rip the jugular and larynx out of Chuck's throat, allowing his lifeless body to drop down hard onto the wet floor. The pool of blood expanded quickly, then thinned as it met the water from the still running showerheads.

Mark got out of bed, whistling as he went into the bathroom to start his day.

Saturday had arrived.

Monday came around much too soon, the weekends seeming shorter all the time now. Mark smiled, remembering the whore he'd picked up on Sunday in the rental car, and all the things he'd been able to do for the first time. His lust had been well satiated, at least for the time being.

He glanced down at the monitor, and clicked on the email button. The latest tirade from his manager, Tessa Marden, about the ongoing quest for higher productivity started a dull throbbing in his temples. He opened his desk drawer and dry swallowed two aspirins from the bottle he kept there, as he deleted the message.

He looked deeply into the stone on the ring and reflected on how he'd fallen into an endless circle of pushing himself harder and harder to satisfy ever increasing targets and to prevent a direct hit on the bullseye he clearly felt on his back. His renewed confidence made him sneer at what a lemming he'd become, and he began planning profound changes for the very near future.

He kept a neutral expression on his face, not wanting anyone to notice anything different about him as he forced himself to get through the rest of the work day.

He turned in early that night, eager to see where his dreams would take him . . . and he soon found himself seated back in his cubicle, at his desk.

The instant messaging application began blinking in the corner of the screen. He clicked on the button, opening the new message.

"Baker. My office, right now," it read, coming from Tessa Marden.

He saved his work and got up, walking to the office in the corner.

"Close the door, Baker."

"What is it, Tessa?" he asked, closing the door behind him.

She got up from behind her desk, holding what appeared to be a spreadsheet printout in her hand.

"I'm getting very tired of constantly reminding you to move faster and get more done. I'm not seeing enough progress here."

"Would you prefer volume or accuracy? I ensure that everything is correct before submitting, you know."

"Don't you dare speak back to me. You'll do what I tell you, or you'll . . ."

The switch had clicked in Mark's head, and he reached up, holding Tessa's head firmly in his hands. She opened her mouth to speak and gasped instead, as his eyes changed from their normal brown color to a fiery red, pulsing in brilliance. He spoke, but it wasn't his voice that came out. This voice was much deeper, very harsh in pitch.

"Listen well, wench. You dare presume that pestilence like you should address *me* in this manner? You will kneel in my presence, you hag!"

Mark pressed her head downward and back, and Tessa fell to her knees hard enough that she heard bones cracking. She started to cry out, but the pressure of his hands on her head increased sharply, the resulting spike of pain causing her to catch her breath instead.

"You have viewed me with scorn for the last time, woman," he said softly, his rough voice much deeper than it had ever been before.

While holding her head, his hands had grown larger, harder, the nails thick and sharp. He pressed his thumbs on her eyes, pushing inward. Her eyes split open easily, offering no resistance, as the thick nails drove through them, through the stems behind them, seeking what lay beyond.

Her blood pooled quickly in the ruined sockets, streaming out and down, rushing into her throat and closing off the scream she'd just begun. She began choking on the blood as the flow increased from the depths his thumbs brutally plunged.

When his nails reached and punctured her frontal lobe, the severe spasms began instantly, her limbs shaking uncontrollably for nearly a full minute, before she fell completely limp within his hands.

He slid his thumbs slowly back out of the bloody eye sockets, let go of her head, letting her fall heavily to the carpeted floor, smiling as he viewed her prone body.

Mark turned over in his sleep, unaware that he was also smiling.

When he arrived at work on Tuesday, he was surprised to find an active crime scene in place, all his co-workers gathered outside the building, not allowed in.

"Mark, did you hear?" Gloria, the HR rep asked him.

"Hear? Hear what?"

"Tessa Marden was murdered last night, right here in the office."

Mark paled a bit, then recovered quickly, "Oh my God, for real?"

"Yes. I heard a couple of the cops talking, and it sounds really nasty."

Mark had a very good idea of just how nasty it had been. The shock and confusion on his face matched well with those of his peers, but in his case, it was from trying to understand how his dream had leaked into reality.

Gloria turned away to answer her cell phone, and spoke quietly for a few minutes. She turned and raised her voice to address the group.

"People? Listen up, please. I just spoke to corporate, and we're to go back home, and not speak to anyone from the press about this at all. We also have to be available for the police, if they want to interview us, so keep your phones handy. Any questions?"

"Yeah, are we getting paid for the day?" a voice from the back asked.

"As far as I know, this will be treated like an emergency, like a weather disaster, so you should be, yes. Just keep your phones handy, like I said, and we'll call everyone with what to do next. Let's get out of here, and let the police do their work."

Mark's mind was racing. He doubted that Ross would have left the wireless signal available, as they'd both left for the day, so he decided to go to the library. He wanted to scan the local news, wanted to check on something.

He walked to the library, and found an empty computer. He entered the guest password, and went to the local news station's website, scrolling down the story headlines, soon finding his fear illustrated on the screen.

"Car salesman found murdered in his home," the headline read. He opened the story and read that Charles Richardson, a car salesman, had been discovered by police at his home when the dealership called, concerned that he hadn't been to work, and wasn't answering his phone. Details were withheld, as it was an active investigation, but an anonymous source told reporters that the crime was "ritualistic" in nature.

So. Chuck, and now Tessa, both brutally murdered, just as he'd dreamed. Yet, he was positive he'd never left his apartment, his bed, so how?

He opened a new tab in the browser, and searched for articles on strange dreams, came across an article on something called "Astral Projection," where spiritualists claimed to project their spirit outward as their body lay in rest. He was certainly no spiritualist, no medium, but what of the demon Asmodeus? Could this be more than just him using his dead uncle's ring as a talisman, a good luck charm to increase his self-confidence with?

"Come on, are you nuts?" he asked himself aloud, earning a disapproving glance from an old timer sitting nearby, reading the newspaper.

He decided to test the theory. He'd go home, and remove the ring, place it back in the box, and close it, as everything had happened after he put it on. If any of this was true, then taking the ring off and sealing it back up should stop, or at least change, the chain of events. He logged out of the computer, got up, and left the library.

It seemed like forever before Mark finally stood up and pulled the signal cord as he approached his stop. The bus pulled over, and he stepped out, walking briskly to his building. Nothing visible in his mailbox, he quickly went up the stairs to his apartment, and closed the door behind him. He sat at the small kitchenette, the box opened in front of him.

He pulled on the ring, but it wouldn't budge. It wouldn't even turn on his finger, feeling frozen in place, and then he heard the deep voice emanating from the bathroom.

"*Tsk, tsk*, Master Baker. You disappoint me so, and I had such high hopes for you."

Frightened now, more like his old self, Mark walked slowly to the open bathroom door, not seeing anyone inside, but that deep voice continued speaking.

"You displayed such promise, much more so than Edgar ever did. And yet, here you are, ready to cast it all aside, to cast *ME* aside."

"Who . . . who's there?" Mark called, his voice shaking.

"Gaze upon me, you pathetic worm!" it commanded. Mark walked into the empty bathroom and looked into the mirror over the sink.

Not reflecting the room any longer, the mirror was filled with dark smoke, swirling slowly around the face of the demon. Blazing red eyes set deep in a hard, chiseled face, it's tongue split and forked as it surfaced between rows of sharp teeth, staring now at Mark with open contempt.

"I offered you everything, exacted vengeance on those who'd wronged you, and still you choose to turn your back on me?"

Mark stuttered weakly, unable to form words, frozen in fear by the vision in the mirror before him.

"Weak, miserable excuse for a mortal, just like the others before you. Let me show you very clearly the choice you have made!"

Hours later, Detectives Joe Bannon and Felix Perez walked up to the apartment building. Bannon glanced at the notebook in his hand.

"Yeah, this is the one. Baker, Mark, lives on the second floor. Let's ring the super to get in."

George responded, buzzing the door, and then walking out to greet them.

"I'm Bannon, this is Perez. We need to talk to one of your tenants, a Mark Baker?"

"Oh yes, Mr. Baker. Good man. He lives up in 2D."

"Is he home now, do you know?"

"I think so. I heard noise up there earlier, like maybe moving something around, but quiet since."

"Let's have a look. Do you have a passkey?"

"Yes, I have all the keys for the building."

They walked up the stairs, and Bannon rang the doorbell, then knocked.

"Mr. Baker? Police. Open the door, we need to talk to you."

The apartment was quiet, no response at all.

"Hey Felix, try his phone, will ya?"

Perez looked at his notebook, and dialed the number. They could hear Mark's cellphone ringing inside.

"Well, his phone is home, anyway. Want to open the door for us?"

George selected the key, and unlocked the door, knocking again as he did.

"Wait here," Bannon said, as he walked inside, Perez right behind him.

George waited in the hallway, wondering what this could be about, when he heard Bannon inside.

"Jesus H. Christ, what a friggin' mess. Felix, call for the meat wagon and the lab rats will ya? This one's even worse than the others."

Felix Perez stepped back from the open bathroom door, desperately trying to hold back the bile that rose so quickly in his throat. The small bathroom was splattered with blood from floor to ceiling, and pieces of Mark Baker were tossed everywhere they looked, completely dismembered.

He hadn't been cut apart, but *torn* apart by something inhumanly strong, the skin jagged, stretched and shredded at the edges.

His head lay in the tub, eyes wide open, an expression of abject terror etched across his face. As bad as the others had been, this one was much more savage, more personal somehow than those were.

Bannon stepped out of the bathroom, looking at his partner.

"Go out and get some air, kid. Can't have you puking all over the crime scene. I'll call it in."

He took out his cell phone, as Perez nodded gratefully and walked to the door.

Neither of them glanced at the small bookshelf or the small, beat up wooden box that sat beside battered paperbacks.

G.A. Miller discovered horror very early on, courtesy of Creature Features on television in the late-1950's/early-1960's. There, he first saw the Universal classic monster movies and many others. As he grew a little older, a friend's brother had a treasure trove of EC Comics from the mid-1950's and this only furthered his fascination. In 1976, he browsed paperbacks at a newsstand, a cover catching his eye. Embossed black, with one spot of color on it: a red drop of blood. It was the first paperback printing of Stephen King's *Salem's Lot*, and it marked his induction as a Constant Reader, a position he still enjoys to this day.

HUNGER

by John Leahy

My friend Edwin Gill was a most annoying person. The reason I found him annoying was because he was good at everything he tried. An excellent athlete, gifted handyman, a guy who could seduce a woman with only a few simple lines, and a brilliant stock trader who infuriatingly only spent about half the time at his desk that I spent slaving at mine. He was also a fan of various high-octane activities like big wave surfing, hang-gliding and rock climbing amidst a host of others. The man was fearless. So, when the terrifying hands erupted from beneath London's tube tunnels, snatching random tube carriages and whisking them back down into whatever unimaginable location in the bowels of the earth that they had emerged from, it didn't surprise me much when Edwin said that he was going down into the hand-hole left between Liverpool Street and Bank. He wanted to see for himself what that hand was attached to.

Edwin was also a brilliant mountain-climber and caver.

The first hand tore through the ground on the Northern Line between Kentish Town and Camden Town. The second one appeared between Elephant and Castle and Kennington and yet still the swarms of London commuters—that hard, creature-of-habit breed—refused to abandon their sacred, high-speed transport. The first hand returned (forensic analysis of CCTV footage had determined that it was indeed that same one as had emerged on the Northern Line) between Knightsbridge and Gloucester Road. By the time the second hand burst forth again between Bank and Liverpool Street, crowds on the tube had diminished by nearly seventy percent. Edwin hadn't been scared, he'd been curious.

So down he'd gone.

I'm looking at two giant . . . things, their huge maws open to receive the screaming people tumbling from the tube carriages that the unspeakable behemoths are holding in their hands. The camcorder footage zooms in on the head of one of the impossible beasts and I can see its dreadful jaws working as it chews on the unfortunates that its mouth contains. Not everything has entered the orifice fully and various human body parts and chunks thereof spill to the ground. The camera descends to the floor of a vast cavern, treating me to the sight of human legs, arms, heads, bits of all the above—some rotting, and parts of skeletons. The view ascends to the thing's head once more. A sickening knot tightens in my gut as my mind grapples with the fantastical nightmare before me. Above the creature's mouth there is no discernible nose, only two small black diamond shapes which I presume are eyes of some sort. And above these, the head ends in what I can only describe as . . . a broccoli-type shape of sorts. The demon's chin is equally grotesque—it is inordinately long, out of all proportion to the being's head—as out of kilter with the whole as are its tiny eyes—and for all the world looks like that of a giant puppet.

The screen goes black.

I look at my old friend in his bed, his hair pure white, his once handsome thirty-year-old face now that of a wizened septuagenarian. His eyes are open, the fear that drove him to his suicide still present in them.

The tube finally stopped running yesterday after the fifth hand incident, which occurred between Bayswater and Notting Hill Gate.

So now the monsters have no more food.

I close Edwin's eyes. I wonder how long it will be before the things under the city can no longer contain their hunger.

I imagine it'll be more than their hands that will be coming up and out of the ground.

John Leahy has had three novels published – *CRO-GIAN*, *The Faith*, and *Unity*. His fourth novel, *Harvest*, is upcoming with Post Mortem Press. He lives in Abbeyfeale, Ireland.

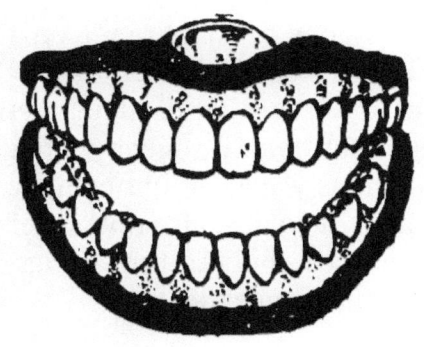

NAILED

by Michelle Mellon

I wouldn't have survived on the colony ships. I'm not just saying that because they wouldn't take me. There's lots of folks who didn't qualify to escape Earth, but really wanted to. Me, I wasn't one of them. I like it here.

Okay, that's not entirely true. I liked things a hell of a lot better before. I guess it'd be more accurate to say I *need* to be here. The dirt and the desperation—without it, I couldn't do what I do to survive.

I toured one of those ships, back in the early days when they were still a promise of things to come. Everything on it looked so neat and contained and sanitary. Not much chance for me to salvage from folks, and I don't have many other skills to offer.

You're young, so you don't know things to be any different. But for these three decades since people have been fleeing this planet, looking for a new home to muddle, we dregs have had to adapt to life on a world that's become little better than a hospice.

Some of us survive better than others. Me, I have a job. You might not think it's much on the surface, and things have obviously gotten, uh, complicated around that recently. Heh. But at least it's not one of those we're--going-to-try-unsuccessfully-to-turn-things-around, blatantly-lie-to-your-face type jobs.

No offense.

Anyway, I'm not important enough to be hated, and not respectable enough to be appreciated. And that's just fine. That means people leave me in peace to do what I need to do: garbage collection.

That's what we used to call it. I know along the way it's gotten many fancier titles; the ones they use to trick us into feeling better about our lot in life. Like they think all of us stuck here on terra firma are dumber than the folks out there in space, and we don't know any better.

Not true. I mean, there are an inordinate number of idiots down here, now that there's been so much culling of the gene pool, but not everyone was left behind because they weren't smart enough. Hell, I even went to college for a while.

But you can call it whatever you want. Garbage collection, waste management, sanitation science—at the end of the day, it's just me cleaning up after other people's messes.

I started with big-time hauls. You know, street stuff. Dumpsters. But the scale was too large for me. My needs are more . . . personal.

Eventually, I worked my way into household management. My specialties were hotels and tenement buildings. Oh, the riches I found in those!

But I'm getting ahead of myself. Or sidetracked, I guess. Maybe not. I mean, that's where it started, so that's just as important as where it all ended up, right?

Anyway, it was much easier after I got the indoor gigs. I could stop scrounging in the waste cans of friends and acquaintances, and rifling through rubbish during the odd office visit.

(Although you'd be surprised what kind of personal things people leave in the office trash. I guess nobody cares anymore, not when it's a race to see who's going to die first—you, or the planet you're "living" on.)

Things were great for a long while. The clients liked how meticulous I was, and I, of course, got my own benefits out of it.

But you're probably wondering why they'd care? Why they'd pay precious money for a cleaning and disposal service, when most of them just used up a site till it was uninhabitable, then move on to another? I mean, no shortage of empty buildings in the world these days.

Well, with all that talk of another colony launch, those business operators knew folks would try to clean up their acts. They want to look respectable in their jobs and find homes that weren't clearly temporary and one step up from the dump. Not going to impress the evaluators if you want a spot on that ship, but you live like a beast among men, huh?

It's been nice, you know, to see people pulled back from the brink of savagery. Not too much of the cream left, which means more curds have a shot to get out this time. Like I said before, though, not for me.

Things were good. I mean, even before the big push to be civilized. Because no matter how down-and-out folks get, there are some things you just gotta take care of. When you don't own a lot, letting a fingernail snag your clothes or a toenail rip through your last pair of socks just won't cut it.

No pun intended.

I see it like this: people had parts they needed to get rid of, and I had a need for those parts. And in those places I worked, there was no shortage of clippings, especially if you devised a sifting system like I did.

I see your face, I get it. Sounds gross. But think about it. Lots of people chew their nails. Me, I've been chewing on my nails since I was a kid. It just got so I needed to supplement my own supply with others.

Hosiery works best, in case you were wondering. You know, for the sifting. Not fishnet stockings, obviously, but if you're lucky enough to find a stretch of pantyhose without holes or snags or bodily fluids on them, it's like panning the trash for gold.

And honestly, that's where it ended for the longest time. I had it totally under control. I'd collect nails and bring them home and snack a bit.

After a while, after eating so many raw, they started getting stuck between my teeth and cutting my gums, you know? That's when I started making a little effort. Marinated them for roasting, or added a sprinkle of something to sauté them with, or worked 'em into recipes. And that was even better.

But I kept getting hungrier. So, I thought, if adding flavor after the fact is this good, how much better would it be to have some "original" flavoring? That's what I call it, anyway. You know, it kinda makes it sound less gruesome.

No?

Well, that first time, that was total happenstance. I know that sounds kinda unbelievable, especially after what I just said about flavoring and all, but that kind of thinking was just fantasy. It's not like I willed anything to happen. I certainly didn't act on my idea. I mean, not at first.

And if I'd known what it would do to me! I mean, we don't have to pretend. I see how you can't stop looking at the extra membrane over my eyes, and my stiff skin, and how my hands are starting to look like split hooves. I call it my "keratin carapace." You gotta laugh, right?

Anyway, it was one of the lower-end hotels, one I hadn't worked before. The kind that's maybe *two* steps above the dump. You should know better than anybody else the kind of bizarre things that happen in this world of ours, new attention to law and order notwithstanding.

I knew something was off when I got in the room, because it was already clean. Like, someone had gone to an extraordinary amount of effort to scrub the place down. There's always places people forget, though. I did my usual crouch-and-bend; searching floor trim and under furniture for things that bounce away and get left behind.

I'm not sure why they didn't think to check under the bed, but there it was. A big toe, barely bloody but newly shorn. Without thinking, I scooped it up. Put it in the special bag I carry for my collecting, added some ice from the machine down the hall, and went about the rest of my morning.

At lunch, I took a little detour home to deposit my find in the fridge. I hardly thought about it the rest of the day. I mean, I was back to my normal collecting habit, going through the usual grind. But that night, well, after that night, there was no going back.

My favorite part of eating meat (when I could get real animal flesh and not this synthetic stuff) was the ribbon of fat. You'd bite into it and get that burst of flavor, and your teeth were happy because they got to chew on something unexpected, attached to that chunk of cow or piece of pig or whatever it was you were eating.

That's how it felt that first time.

I tossed that toe in the oven, thinking it'd be like when you baste a turkey and the skin's crackly and tasty. Except when I went to carve away the nail, it didn't come off cleanly.

You know how nails sit on that flat pad of flesh? The nail bed, they call it. There's also this special area that feeds the whole deal. The matrix. Well, this bit hanging on to the nail was a bit of bed and a bit of matrix, curled up and crunchy-looking.

Sounds funny, considering where I was at that point, but I was actually a little bit squeamish about it. I got over it real quick, though. I mean, the smell of it, and the pool of saliva threatening to drown me, well, they decided the matter.

I shrugged and popped it all—nail and tiny shreds of meat—in my mouth. I don't even know how to describe it. Chewy with a bit of salty tang, and then the quick crunch of flesh. You've never tasted anything so extraordinary.

I tried to ignore the cravings. I really did. But every time I sifted some nails into a pan or a casserole dish, I thought about how much better they'd taste with some meat attached. I'd known for a long time I couldn't stop my nail addiction, and now I realized I couldn't go back to the way things had been before.

Nothing hasty, though. I thought it out first. Made a plan, targeted legitimate sources. You know, nobody gets hurt, no harm, no foul. I lobbied for cleanup on the hospital and clinic rounds. Those included the morgues. It seemed like the perfect fit.

In fact, that worked for a while, but then I guess somebody noticed that digits went missing on my shifts.

Nobody said anything official about it, but I was moved back to working among the living.

What to do now? I had a craving that I couldn't control. I mean, at this point, I didn't even want to control it. But the live ones would be too much trouble. Half of them were trying to get themselves fit enough to get on that fabled colony ship, and the other half were scrappy survivors like me.

I decided to go after the nearly dead. You know, the ones clogging up alleys and doorways with their disease and depression and destitution. They won't work, they don't care, and they won't die right away. It seemed wasteful to let useful limbs sit around being useless.

I noticed a garden shed on the way to work one day, and that's where I found the knife. It was some abandoned apartment complex that was probably real nice way back when, with manicured strips of grass and bushes they trimmed into animals or fancy shapes. Now it's just a shell, like so much of the city, and the tools were in there for the taking.

I considered the shears first, but figured they'd be more work to get back into shape. When I saw the machete, I knew that was it. It took about a week before I had scrubbed off all the rust and had it sharpened up, ready to go.

Still, I was nervous. I mean, you think I was all callous and single-minded about this, but that wasn't the way it was at all. It was another few days before I could work up enough nerve to go after my first one.

Long story short, it was clumsy and messy, but at the end of it, I had twenty delectable tidbits, and there was one less undesirable clogging the streets.

The details? Sure, I remember. Funny how with food and sex you remember that first time. Makes you think, right?

Anyway, there was an alley near one of my jobs where the derelicts liked to hang out. It was quiet, a bit off the beaten path, and there was only one active building in the area using the dumpsters nearby, so no real threat of interruption.

If you watch long enough, you'll see the rhythms and habits of those folks, same as anyone else. That's how I knew there was a stretch each night when a few of them went off to scavenge in those dumpsters, and left one behind to guard their home base.

There wasn't much to the guy, either physically or mentally. Still, I didn't want to take my chances being surprised at the last minute. I threw something—a can or a rock—to get him to look into the far end of the alley. Then I swooped in behind him and beheaded him with the machete.

Of course, it didn't go as smoothly as it does when you just say it like that. I mean, they make it look so easy in the movies.

Well, yeah, I guess you wouldn't know anything about that.

But even on a scrawny guy like that one, there's a lot of tissue and bone and stringy bits to get through. I had to hack at him a bit until he went down for good. Luckily, he didn't make much noise. After that, I chopped off his fingers and toes. That was a damn sight easier than the head, let me tell you. And I hightailed it out of there.

It got easier as I went along. I had that knife sharpened and shining, and I practiced my swing so it'd take less effort, and I was feeling good for an old dog my age. Stronger, even, like this was the right path for me and it'd just been waiting for me to find it.

Until that last one.

Looking back, I totally ignored the signs. What can I say? I got greedy. I mean, she was in the wrong place, for sure. But she was alert and relatively well-dressed and she had these little round fingers. You could almost call them plump.

So yeah, I should have known better. I let my hunger take over, till all my senses revolved around the need for that flavory crunch and crackle.

At this point, I had probably taken down thirty or so derelicts, all of them much larger than her. It must have been the effect of the matrix I was eating. I mean, these physical changes for sure. Made me doubly glad I'd gone for the machete instead of the shears, what with my hands morphing like they are.

But mentally, too. Like the matrix was feeding my desire, just like it had fed all those fingers and toenails. I felt strong and confident. So confident, with that last one, that when I struck at her and missed, I was too shocked to realize she was agile enough to keep dodging me and maybe even fight back.

It even took me a little while to realize she had been crying out the whole time. Screaming bloody murder at the top of her lungs. It unsettled me a bit, and I missed my next two swings. But I realized she wouldn't get much help in this part of the city, which calmed me for another attack.

Of course, what I didn't know was that it was trendy now to set up clubs in the run-down districts, and that's where she'd been, and that's where the cavalry came from.

So here I am. No point denying any of it. I mean, a crowd of folks came from around the corner and saw me facing off with her, machete in hand. I cut some of 'em pretty good before I went down, but down I went.

And I'm sure you've already been to my place and found my leftovers from yesterday. Usually I make sure to clean up any evidence before I leave for the day. You know, just in case. But I think I was just too distracted, thinking ahead to the next opportunity. That last set wasn't satisfying—a little grainy, even. The guy might've had a fungus.

Anyway, that's it. I don't have anything else to say.

The ones in between? Sorry, I don't remember much about them. I know it sounds horrible, but it really felt like the whole plan was a win-win scenario. Less folks stuck between the cracks for the city to deal with, more treats for me.

But I do have a question. What happens next? I mean, this is kinda new territory for you in this weird, post-post world of ours. Trials are old-fashioned, jails are expensive, official executions are outlawed. What happens to me now?

Nah, I'm in no hurry. I got all the time in the world to wait for a decision. Where else am I going to go? Besides, that holding cell is pretty damn comfortable compared to the place I was living. Although I noticed you guys do it old-school around here, huh?

Oops, sorry. Didn't mean to bump into you like that. I know it just looks like my body is shellacked into some kind of weird toy-soldier stiffness, but it's getting harder to sense where it is in the world.

The changes, they're accelerating much faster now. Maybe it's the stress. Not about what I've done, no. About who I'm becoming.

What I mean is, I'm still under here. I still have my memories of the times before, and how I felt when the last people I cared about either left on one of those ships, or died at the hands of this miserable world.

But it's like I'm wearing a me-shaped shell or something, and I'm trying to figure out how to move around in it, and keep thinking my own thoughts, and hold on to a little bit of who I used to be.

Anyway, I'm not looking for sympathy. That'd be a tough one to sell at this point, huh? I guess all that sitting and running off at the mouth just made me a bit stiff and clumsy. Here, let me help you gather up all these keys.

There you go. So, back to my cell, then? Yeah, like I was saying, it's much cleaner and cozier than the place I used to call home. One drawback, though—the food's not as good. *Ha ha.*

Speaking of, did anyone ever tell you, officer, you have the loveliest fingers?

Michelle Mellon has been published in several horror and science fiction anthologies. In August 2015, she and her husband relocated from San Francisco to Germany, where Ms. Mellon is a stay-at-home mom to their cat while she works on a horror story collection and writes a blog about living overseas.

ALIEN: COVENANT and the Search for Ridley Scott

A Gehenna Post Review

(Originally Published in the Gehenna Post)

Nearly 40 years ago, 38 to be precise, audiences were stunned with a film that would not only spawn a franchise, but also create an entire science fiction legacy, atop of the fire that it would breathe into the life of one director's career–none other than Ridley Scott, who would go on to craft such films as *Blade Runner* (1982) and *Gladiator* (2000). The film aforementioned was his masterpiece, *Alien* (1979). Though the love for the film initially was not nearly the peak at which it is today, the film still effected a lot of people and brought passion into exploring the darker sides of science fiction. Without *Alien*, there would have never been *Aliens* (1986), no *Event Horizon* (1997), no *Predator* (1987) Pandorum (2009), no John Carpentr's *The Thing* (1982), the list goes on.

Fast forward to 1986 and James Cameron, who would go on to direct *Terminator 2: Judgment Day* (1991) and *Avatar* (2009), took the helm from Scott and gave us *Aliens*, a film possibly neck-and-neck with Scott's original vision. Then the journey withered a bit as sequel after sequel released with none of the same passion that Scott and Cameron put into the franchise. Not until a few decades later, when audiences were given *Prometheus* (2012). Critics can say what they will about *Prometheus*–most complaints deriving from its lack of Xenomorphs–but the film was unique. Scott wanted to create a universe that was not reliant on his iconic beasts. He wanted to delve into the mythology and show that the world could stand on its own without giant phallic monsters tearing people apart. More than anything, his idea and concept to explore alien creatures that created mankind, was exhilarating and refreshing in a genre that, as of late, seemed to rely on Michael Bay action and special effects.

When it was announced a few years back that the sequel to *Prometheus* would be titled *Prometheus: Paradise Lost*, many fans were excited. We would see the home world of the engineers! We would find all the answers surrounding the mystery of our creation. A whole new planet, ecosystem, civilization, and culture awaited us on Paradise and we were enthralled to experience it. Yet somewhere along pre-production, something happened. Ridley Scott announced the change of title to *Alien: Covenant* (2017) and spoke further and further on the film being more directly related to the *Alien* franchise. It appeared to many that Scott did not like the backlash received for his decisions for *Prometheus* and wanted to cater to audiences more than stay true to his craft and vision.

Many interviews and quotes from Ridley Scott erupted throughout the past two years leading up to *Covenant* that had many fans worried. From his interview with the Sydney Morning Herald, where he told the interviewer that he wanted to do up to six more *Alien* films, to his interview with Express, where he stated that he would consider having a CGI de-aged Sigourney Weaver (Ellen Ripley) in future films, it seemed that Scott's desire for box office numbers outweighed his passion for creating artistic interpretations of this universe. The 79-year-old may be encroaching upon the end of his life, hoping to relish in any success he can muster. Considering the untimely death of his brother Tony Scott in 2012, the same year *Prometheus* released, it wouldn't be crazy to think that Scott might be experiencing a crisis of sorts as far as his own mortality is concerned.

Nevertheless, *Alien: Covenant* holds none of the wonder that *Alien, Aliens,* and *Prometheus* boasted. A gory action bonanza that shallows in the terms of character development and festers inside of plot holes, the film not only feels underwhelming throughout its second and third acts, but it also spells a saddening fate for a beloved franchise. In the previous three films listed above, audiences cared about the characters, felt their pain. From Ellen Ripley and her stunning transformation to badass heroine, to Elizabeth Shaw (Noomi Rapace) and her unbelievable perseverance, Scott has shown an incredible talent of portraying lead characters that science fiction fans not only love, but want to see more of. Even in recent memory, with Scott's Oscar-nominated science fiction film *The Martian* (2015), based on the novel of the same name by Andy Weir, Matt Damon received many nominations and accolades for his titular role, further proving Scott's ability to create memorable characters. No characters in *Alien: Covenant* had these aspects, not even David (Michael Fassbender) who was the standout performance of *Prometheus*, had nearly the amount of charm that the character is capable of possessing. Even the synthetic felt ... well ... synthetic.

The opening act of *Alien: Covenant* was thematically relative to *2001: A Space Odyssey* (1968). The stunning visual effects were breathtaking and the technology so advanced yet believable. Initially, it was with much pleasure that the film felt as though it were going in a direction that would grasp the audience's attention and thrill with the same mysterious and terrifying deep space themes that riddled the original two *Alien* films and *Prometheus.* By the time the second act starts, the movie steps into puddles of tropes consistently, becoming formulaic and hollow. Part of what made Scott's *Alien* so effective when it first came out, was the fact that the little bit of blood and gore that was in the long run time was depicted discreetly and/or effectively. *Alien: Covenant* has over-the-top gore that becomes so ridiculous at points that fans may find themselves laughing at the absurdity before them. Ridley Scott has always made bloody films, but this may be the first time he made a film that was bloody for the sake of being bloody. The CGI of the Xenomorphs and their relatives compare to CGI from 2004, consistently pulling viewers out of the universe as compared to *Prometheus* which was a visual spectacle in every way, the few instances of creature CGI always authentic and believable.

As far as plot, the story unfolds in an interesting way early on but quickly falls into pits of lazy plot devices and tropes that are identical to previous installments. As soon as the crew of the Covenant vessel land on the foreign planet, the film nosedives into a poor-written oblivion. The dialogue is boring and any efforts at character development are either emotionless, lazy, or briefly explored before being dropped off completely. There are several moments in the film's climax that will make fans of the Alien franchise think to themselves, "Are you serious?" Despite a few interesting plot twists, the film ends with–start drum roll–a setup for a sequel.

There was a time when Ridley Scott was respected for his passion and ability to craft beautiful landscapes with remarkable characters. Now, this aspect of the legendary director seems to be faded, filling his most loyal fans with disappointment. There were two possible titles for this review that we considered before sitting down to watch Alien: Covenant, the first being Alien: Revenant (with hopes that the film would revitalize the franchise even further), the second being Alien: Covenant and the Search for Ridley Scott. Clearly the latter was chosen and the title holds true.

Where is Ridley Scott? What happened to one of science fiction's most beloved directors? Will we find him again? Clearly Scott vanished during the directing of this film, because not a single aspect, despite the cinematography, echoes of the legendary filmmaker we have all come to love so dearly over the past four decades.

RATING: 2/5 STARS

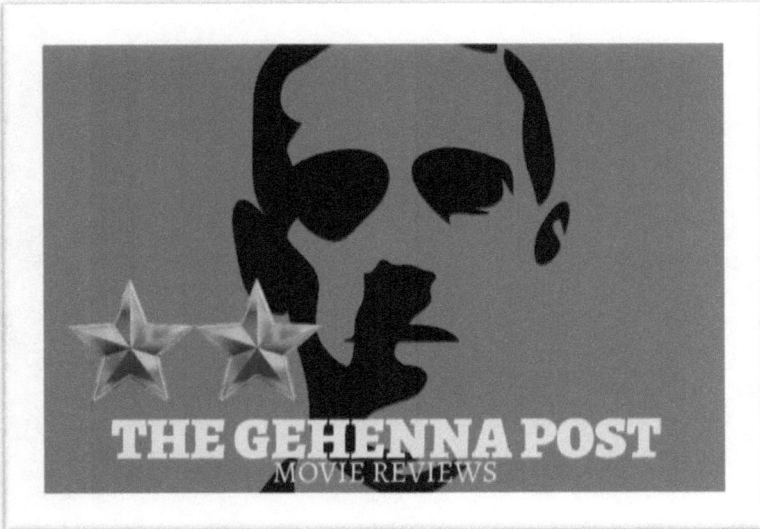

Don't miss the new novel from Bram Stoker Award-nominated author, James Dorr!

Buy it on Amazon today!
If you enjoyed **Hinnom Magazine**, make sure to leave a review on Amazon and follow us on social media!

Facebook: www.facebook.com/gehennaandhinnom-books
Twitter: www.twitter.com/GehennaBooks
Website: www.gehennaandhinnom.wordpress.com

Look out for our new releases in 2017!

June 30th, 2017

Hinnom Magazine Issue 001

August 31st, 2017

Hinnom Magazine Issue 002

September 22nd, 2017

Year's Best Body Horror 2017 Anthology

October 31st, 2017

Hinnom Magazine Issue 003

November 22nd, 2017

Year's Best Transhuman SF 2017 Anthology

December 31st, 2017

Hinnom Magazine Issue 004

www.ingramcontent.com/pod-product-compliance
Lightning Source LLC
Chambersburg PA
CBHW020636130626
46552CB00003B/1255